DREW AND THE HOMEBOY QUESTION

STEVIE

HUDDLES ME KENNY

Also by Robb Armstrong

Drew and the Bub Daddy Showdown

Jump Start: A Love Story

DREW AND THE HOMEBOY QUESTION

by Robb Armstrong

HarperTrophy®
A Division of HarperCollins Publishers

Drew and the Homeboy Question
Copyright © 1997 by Robb Armstrong
All rights reserved. No part of this book may be used or reproduced in any manner
whatsoever without written permission
except in the case of brief quotations embodied in critical articles
and reviews. Printed in the United States of America.
For information address HarperCollins Children's Books,
a division of HarperCollins Publishers,
10 East 53rd Street, New York, NY 10022.

Library of Congress Cataloging-in-Publication Data
Armstrong, Robb.
    Drew and the homeboy question / written and illustrated by Robb Armstrong
      p.   cm.
    Summary: Drew's oldest friends accuse him of snobbery when he wins a scholarship
to the Deerwood Academy for Boys, an exclusive all-white school.
    ISBN 0-06-027527-8 (lib. bdg.) — ISBN 0-06-442047-7 (pbk.)
    1. Afro-Americans—Juvenile fiction. [1. Afro-Americans—Fiction. 2. Race
relations—Fiction. 3. Schools—Fiction.] I. Title.
PZ7.A73385Dt   1997   96-41319
[Fic]—dc20   CIP
                                                                                   AC

Design by Alison Donalty
1   2   3   4   5   6   7   8   9   10
❖
First Edition

For Sherry, my wonderful wife,
whose intense love and commitment
made this book possible.

Chapter
1

The day Skipper pulled the trigger in the schoolyard of Drummond Junior High School, he changed my life forever.

The bullet didn't hit me. I was five blocks away at Hamilton Elementary School. Still, the bullet had a profound impact on my life. It also had quite an impact on Vice Principal Warren's car.

Skipper was in a corner of Drummond's schoolyard. He was showing Wolfman and Fat Ernie how to handle a loaded gun, when he accidentally fired it. The bullet shattered two windows in Mr. Warren's empty station wagon. It also blew off Skipper's pinkie finger.

People were calling Drummond a bad school long before Skipper's gun went off. Kids in the neighborhood had been trading war stories about Drummond for at least three years. Recently, parents had begun to trade stories too.

When Skipper fired that gun, I had no idea it would affect me. My best friends, Stevie, Huddles, and Kenny, laughed about it. So did I.

None of us liked Skipper much. We all felt that he had gotten exactly what he deserved for waving that stupid gun around.

As it turned out, my chances of attending Drummond Junior High were shot away right along with Skipper's pinkie.

STEVIE'S MOM

MY MOM →

ME, EAVESDROPPING.

The next day I heard my mom talking with Stevie's mom on the phone.

"Drew is going into the seventh grade next year, and I absolutely refuse to send him to Drummond," Mom said. "That school is a disgrace!"

This was too good to miss. I ran upstairs and picked up the extension phone so I could listen in.

"I *have* to send Stevie there," said Mrs. Bishop. "I don't have much choice."

3

"Have you ever thought about private school?"

"Private schools cost too much money, Doris," said Stevie's mom. "Besides, we pay taxes so that our children can get a decent education. Don't we?"

"Well, a good education is worth the extra money," said Mom.

"Some of those private schools cost more than college," said Mrs. Bishop.

"They have scholarships, Sarah! Our kids are smart and talented. And I've heard they need black kids badly!" Mom answered.

I quietly hung up the extension. I was confused. Why would private schools "need black kids badly"? I didn't like the sound of that. Were they using black kids for some weird experiments or something?

There's no way I'm going to some stupid private school anyway, I thought. I'd go to Drummond—like Kyle, my older brother.

I didn't know it then, but Kyle was the last Taylor kid Drummond would ever see.

4

Chapter 2

There had been other stories about Drummond, but the one about Skipper and the gun was different. It actually ran in the *Tribune*, a real city newspaper. There was a photo of Skipper, holding a heavily bandaged hand over his face, and a huge headline that read SHOOTING AT DRUMMOND. Then, in much smaller letters, it said, STUDENT LOSES A FINGER.

That same week, Mom and Dad began looking into private schools for me to attend in the fall.

Meanwhile, I had more important things on my mind—like my latest comic book masterpiece. I couldn't wait to show it to Stevie,

Kenny, and Huddles. They were my best friends. They were also my biggest fans. Every time I drew a comic book starring Mason Stone, Superagent, they flipped through the pages eagerly. Their loud, cheerful approval of every drawing meant a lot to me.

On Saturday morning I ran outside to find Stevie sitting on my front steps. Huddles was across the street. He was talking to a girl named Felicia.

"Check it out," I said, handing Stevie the comic book. "Issue Number Ten!"

"Um-hmm," said Stevie, without much interest. He riffled through the pages but didn't really look at them. He kept glancing over at Huddles and Felicia.

"You aren't reading it!" I exclaimed.

"Sorry, Drew," said Stevie. "I'm a little distracted."

"By Felicia?"

"No, by Huddles," he answered. "He just told me he's getting left back."

"*What?*" I sat down on the steps, shocked.

"Huddles isn't going to graduate. He's got to stay at Hamilton next year while we go to Drummond."

"Get out of here!" I couldn't believe this news. "How could Huddles fail sixth grade? He's too smart!"

This was true. In fact, up until the third grade, Huddles was getting straight A's. He was what we used to call a brainiac—super-intelligent and nerdy. He even wore thick glasses. But, when he was nine and his parents split up, Huddles changed. He stopped caring about his grades and produced only enough to get by. No more A's. No more thick glasses. He became "cool."

I knew Huddles was still a closet brainiac. Even if he spent all his time goofing around, he was still the smartest kid on my block.

"Ask him," said Stevie. "But don't tell him I told you anything."

Across the street, Felicia walked away from Huddles. He stood there waiting. Then

he came over and sat down next to me on the steps. He nudged me with his elbow. "Yo," he said. "That chick want to get with me."

"Who? Felicia?" I asked, widening my eyes. Stevie burst out laughing.

"Felicia?" he bellowed. "Ha ha haw gck gck gck!" Stevie's laughter was always loud and mocking, with a weird gagging sound at the end that escaped through the gaps in his huge front teeth. "Gck gck gck!"

It was awful for the victim, and hilariously funny to everyone else.

"What's so funny?" asked Huddles, annoyed.

"*You're* funny!" Stevie chuckled. "You've been trying to rap to Felicia for two years! She ain't thinking about you, 'cause you're smelly and you've chewed off all your fingernails!" Stevie laughed again, so hard he nearly fell off the stoop.

"Yeah," I joined in. "But miracles do happen. You might get lucky if Felicia loses her sense of smell."

Stevie rolled off the stoop and fell to the pavement howling with laughter, gagging and holding his stomach. "Gck gck gck!"

I waited for Huddles to come back with a stream of insults about us and our families. He didn't do that. Instead, he put his head down in his lap and began to cry.

At first I thought he was putting us on. So did Stevie. He kept shouting with laughter. "Gck gck gck!" He didn't realize Huddles was really crying.

"Stevie, shut up!" I yelled. "Something's wrong." Something *was* wrong. Huddles wasn't the crying type; he was the king of the funny put-down. His wit was lightning quick, and his tongue was razor sharp. I could draw. Stevie could too. Kenny could do karate. Huddles could put you down. He'd never cried in front of any of us before.

"Huddles, man . . . what's wrong?" I asked, draping an arm around him.

His shoulders shook, and he blurted out, "I'm getting left back!"

12

"For real?" I asked.

"See? I told you!" said Stevie.

"Shut your big mouth, Stevie!" said Huddles without a trace of his usual playfulness.

"Here comes Kenny," I said. "Cool out for a minute."

Kenny was wearing a black kung fu outfit complete with black slippers from Chinatown. He was chewing on a huge wad of Bub Daddy bubble gum.

Kenny took karate lessons. He had watched so many Bruce Lee movies that he was convinced he was Chinese, even though he was black, like the rest of us. Sometimes he even spoke a few words of Chinese, but now he spoke English.

"What's wrong with Hud?" he asked, knitting his eyebrows together.

"I'm getting left back! You guys will all be together at Drummond next year, and I'll still be at Hamilton!" Huddles choked out.

We'd been best friends in the same school,

sometimes in the same class, since the first grade. Now Stevie and I fell silent. Kenny stopped blowing his Bub Daddy bubbles. No one said a word, but we all sensed that our friendship was being tested for the first time. Huddles and Kenny walked away without even looking at my comic book.

"Can I take it home to read later?" asked Stevie.

"You'd better return it fast. It's my only copy," I said.

"No problem," said Stevie. "I'll get it right back to you."

Mom and Dad called a family meeting at seven o'clock that night.

After dinner, Kyle and my older sister, Jessie, cleared the table. Then Mom and Dad spread several brochures and pamphlets on it.

"Kids," said Dad. "Your mother and I have decided to send Drew to a private school in the fall."

"To develop his art and writing," added Mom.

"Now, I know this might sound unfair to you, Jessie, and you, Kyle," said Dad apologetically, "but your mother and I . . ."

"Feel that Drew has a unique gift," finished Mom.

"Pop, it's cool with me," said Kyle. "I would hate for my little brother to end up at Drummond, anyway."

Dad and I looked at each other, surprised.

I had heard Dad's fond memories of Drummond ever since I could remember. He still wore a once-maroon cutoff sweatshirt that had faded to an odd shade of pink with DRUMMOND XL in huge white letters across the front.

And he always bragged about his glory days at the school. He was especially fond of his basketball teammates. He kept in touch with some of them, and others had gone on to fame and fortune.

"Decky Hightower played center for the

Drummond Wildcats," he'd say whenever the Florida State coach appeared on national television.

Another schoolmate, Renaldo Watts, played pro ball after high school, then parlayed his earnings into a multimillion-dollar software business. Dad talked about Renaldo whenever the subject of money came up.

Now Dad looked hurt, and so did I. I wanted to follow in his footsteps. Kyle's footsteps too. Jessie had a different reaction.

"I don't think it's fair that Drew the Wonderboy gets special treatment! I want to get out of Drummond too!" she squealed.

"Well, Jessie," said Dad, "we intend to have you enrolled in Little Rose in the fall."

Her jaw dropped.

"Little Rose? That Catholic school for girls? We aren't even Catholic!" she protested. "And that uniform—I hate that stupid tunic!" She slammed both hands on the table for effect.

"Little Rose is an excellent school, Jessie! Much better than Drummond!" said Mom. "You might like it. Oh . . . and Rochelle will be going there too."

Jessie's face brightened instantly. Rochelle was one of her best friends.

"So which one of these brochures am I going to?" I frowned.

"Don't sound so thrilled," Mom said, lifting an eyebrow.

"It's not like we're sending you off to jail," said Dad. "These are pretty fancy schools here," he added.

"We're not sure where you'll be going, son. It depends on how well you do in the entrance exams," said Mom.

"I've gotta take tests?" I groaned.

"It'll be easy, Drew." Mom tried to reassure me.

"If it was easy, they wouldn't call it a test," commented Kyle.

"Yeah," said Jessie. "They'd call it a 'game.'"

"Or an 'activity' or an 'exercise,'" I agreed.

"Well, it'll seem easy to you, son," said Dad, patting my arm. "You're our little genius."

Kyle reached over and patted my arm, too, as if to reinforce Dad's praise. But Jessie sat there and shook her head knowingly.

She got on my nerves a lot, but Jessie knew me better than anyone in the family.

"Dad is totally delusional," she said to me quietly.

Jessie was in touch with my insecurities. She knew that Dad was wrong about my being a genius.

She knew that I was petrified.

Chapter 3

As we completed the one-hour journey from my close-knit city neighborhood to the rolling hills of Deerwood, one question rang in my mind.

"Where are we?"

It seemed as if we had left the United States entirely. Our modest little blue hatchback with the squeaky axle had bounded noisily up the interstate with the whole family inside. We'd sung old songs. We'd laughed loudly at each other's corny jokes. But as we approached the campus of the Deerwood School for Boys, we all fell silent. Even Dad looked awed. He hunched over the steering wheel, craning his neck to see the tops of the tallest evergreens that ever lined a driveway.

Then we entered through huge iron gates,

under an imposing sign bearing the school's name.

Suddenly the squeaking of the little blue hatchback's axle became loud and embarrassing.

"When are you going to get that fixed, Dad?" I whispered from the backseat.

"Tomorrow," he said as the car crept along the endless driveway.

"Now, *this* is a school!" said Mom.

"It is?" whispered Kyle.

"Honey, you just passed a parking spot," said Mom.

The white gravel crunched beneath our tires as Dad backed into a parking space between two dark green vans.

"We're here," he said, as if we hadn't noticed.

A wide staircase led us up to a huge gray stone building with an inscription carved above the doorway. I wasn't sure if it was Latin or Greek. All I knew was that I couldn't understand it.

The reception hall, a massive room, was lined floor to ceiling in dark mahogany. Our footsteps echoed as we strolled through it like tourists.

Portraits of well-heeled men stared down at us from the walls. Big porcelain urns sprouted lush bouquets of fresh flowers.

The huge hall was empty except for the five of us—and a skinny white kid standing at the foot of a sweeping staircase.

The boy seemed to be about my age, but he had a smaller build. He had very dark hair framing a pale face and he wore badly wrinkled clothes. As we came in he was digging through his pants pockets and the pockets of the balled-up blue blazer he was carrying.

While my family studied the oil paintings in the grand hall, I watched him. He saw me and smiled.

"Hey," I said. "I'm Drew Taylor. Do you go here?"

"Actually, no. I'm only visiting," he said, still searching his pockets. "Darnedest

23

thing. I had some cash this morning to buy my train ticket home, and it's vanished."

"My parents are right over there," I said. "They'll give you some money for the train."

"Don't be absurd," he said, forcing a grin. He looked really embarrassed. "We don't even know one another."

"You know me. I'm Drew Taylor," I repeated.

"Quartie Portnoy," he said, reaching out to shake my hand.

"Corey?" I asked.

"No, Quartie. As in the fourth. I'm Harrison Portnoy the Fourth. My nickname is Quartie."

"Oh, I get it." I had never heard anything so ridiculous in my life. *How can this poor kid go through life with a nickname like that?* I wondered.

"I think I'll take you up on that offer," he said suddenly. "I've definitely lost my five."

I got a ten from my mom and gave it to Quartie.

"This is too kind," he said. "I'll repay you someday."

"Not much of a chance that we'll see each other again," I told him. "I'll never get into a school like this."

"Then why don't you give me your mailing address?"

"We're in the midtown phone book, under 'Reginald Taylor.' "

"Good," he said, smiling. "I'll look you up when I've got the money."

"Don't worry about it," I said. "It's no big deal."

"Well, thanks, Drew Taylor," he called as I rejoined my parents. "I won't forget this."

Dad beamed at me.

"It was nice of you to talk with that boy," he said. "That's how you'll make friends once you get in. By taking the initiative!"

"*If* he gets that scholarship," said Mom.

"Did you just give that white boy ten dollars?" asked Jessie.

"No," said Mom. "Drew said the boy

needed a couple of dollars for the train. Where's my change, son?"

"I don't have any change. I gave him the whole ten," I said.

"Are you out of your mind!" Dad exclaimed. "You can't go around giving away ten-dollar bills, Drew!"

Jessie stifled a laugh.

"That kid was poor," I said. "Did you see how he was dressed?"

"He wouldn't be here if he was poor," said Kyle.

"*We're* here," I protested.

"Forget it, everybody," said Mom. "It's okay to give to the poor. Hopefully the scholarship committee will feel that way about us."

Chapter
4

We were at Deerwood that day to meet with Dr. Barnett, the dean of admissions. A tall man with a gray beard, he came into the hallway and greeted us warmly.

Dr. Barnett was dressed completely in green and blue. He wore a green blazer with antlers embroidered on the pocket, a blue shirt, and a green-and-blue striped tie. I remembered reading that green and blue were the Deerwood colors. As I looked around, I saw them on just about everything. Even the earth and sky seemed to cooperate with Barnett and his plans for a campus tour.

This man truly loved the Deerwood School for Boys. And that was what he called it—he never once shortened it to "Deerwood." Every time he uttered the words *The Deerwood*

School for Boys, he breathed through them and rolled his eyes as if the magnificence of the school was making him light-headed.

Dr. Barnett also loved every accomplishment of the student body. He listed each achievement as if he were bragging about his own children.

"Our literary magazine, *The Beacon*, has won first prize for excellence from the National Council of Secondary School Literary Magazine Editors. That's the third year in a row," he breathed.

"Um-hmm," murmured Dad, trying to act interested.

"Are you rich?" asked Jessie suddenly, much to the embarrassment of my folks.

"I love teaching," he answered a little stiffly. "But I must confess that if my motivation for doing so was strictly financial, I would probably be engaged in something utterly different." He chuckled after saying this, but none of us got the joke. I still wondered if he was rich.

← Dr. Barnett.
Weird, huh?

"How many students are enrolled here?" asked Mom.

"The Middle House, where Drew would be enrolled, has a student body of one hundred and fifty. Each of his classes would average fifteen students. Merion Prep, our rival school, averages double this amount," he said proudly.

Why is he so proud of Deerwood for having fewer students than Merion Prep? I thought. *Their rival school is in the lead!*

"Who decided to build this school so far away from everything?" asked Kyle.

"Somebody around here must be crazy about the color green," said Jessie.

"How often do the commuter trains run?" asked Mom.

"Um-hmm," said Dad.

"How many minority students go here?" asked Kyle.

"Currently, our diversity efforts have produced three percent enrollment for students of color," said Dr. Barnett.

"How many black kids is that?" asked Jessie.

"One of our finest students graduated last year. Ronald Walker was captain of our winning lacrosse team. He was a chemistry and Latin major who is now in his freshman year at Yale. We are very proud of him!"

"So now that he's gone—" began Kyle.

"How many black kids are left?" finished Jessie.

"Kids," said Dad. "Let your mother and me ask the questions around here, hmm?"

"How many black kids are left?" asked Mom.

"Well, if Drew enrolls here," said Dr. Barnett, "we will have one black student again!"

30

Chapter

5

"You broke Fat Ernie's nose?" I gasped.

"He's lucky that's all I did," said Kyle. He took a huge bite of his peanut butter and banana sandwich. We were sitting in the kitchen after school, a week after our trip to Deerwood.

"That guy could get you into real trouble," I said, frowning.

"I'm already suspended," Kyle reminded me. "How much more trouble could I get into?"

"What if Fat Ernie tries to get you back? What if . . . ?"

We looked at each other without saying a word. Everybody in the neighborhood knew that Fat Ernie had Skipper's gun. He'd taken it after the finger incident.

Fat Ernie had told so many people that he

had the gun, we all wondered why he both-
ered to hide it at all. Why didn't he just dis-
play it on his front porch under a flashing
neon sign that said I'VE GOT SKIPPER'S GUN
NOW!

"You think he'll come after me with the
gun?" said Kyle, as if he was asking if I
thought it would rain. I never could understand how a person could go through life
without any fear whatsoever, but Kyle did
just exactly that.

Fat Ernie, on the other hand, boasted
about the gun for the same reason Skipper
had carried it—to scare people. Ernie figured that nobody would ever take a swing at
him as long as he made it known that he was
armed and dangerous.

"I'll bet he never thought I'd punch his
lights out." Kyle grinned.

"Why'd you do it?"

"He was going around calling you a white
boy," said my brother angrily.

"What's so terrible about that?"

"They're trying to kick you out of the black race! Jessie told everyone about our trip to Deerwood last week. Now Fat Ernie, Rock, Wolfman, and Crazy Cecil are all talking behind your back. They're telling everybody at school that we're a bunch of snobs. They're saying you think you're too good for Drummond."

"It's just talk. Dad always says talk is cheap, right? It's not worth fighting about," I reasoned.

"They're not just talking. They broke into my locker and sprayed WHITE BOY inside it," said Kyle.

"What?" I yelled.

Kyle calmly poured another glass of milk and took a sip. "They shouldn't have done that," he said. "Plus they stole my new sneakers."

"So what did you do? Just walk up to Fat Ernie and punch him?"

"I asked him to take off my sneakers and give them back. He was in the boys' room

33

with Crazy Cecil and Rock, trying to act tough. He laughed at me. Said Mom gave him the sneakers."

"*Our* Mom?" I said, appalled. "He talked about *Mom*?"

"That was when I stopped talking and started punching," said Kyle. "Two shots square in his nose. The blood got all over his Chicago Bulls T-shirt."

"What did Cecil and them do?"

"What do you think they did? They ran. Those guys only *talk* tough. They're cowards."

"So now you're suspended, and Mom and Dad have to go to Drummond and meet with the principal." I shook my head. "What a mess."

"So what?" said Kyle. "Fat Ernie gave me back my sneakers."

Jessie and her big mouth started this, I thought. *Who else has she told?*

Chapter

6

I found out the next day.

After school Stevie, Huddles, and Kenny cornered me in the playground.

"Why didn't you tell us you wouldn't be at Drummond next year?" yelled Stevie.

"Yeah! We had to hear it from your sister!" shouted Kenny.

"At least somebody in your family is telling us what's going on," said Huddles, biting his mangled thumbnail.

"Listen, the reason I didn't say anything is because I probably won't even get in," I said. "I still gotta take a bunch of really hard exams. I'll probably fail."

"Jessie says they love you out there," accused Kenny. "Gave you the red carpet treatment."

"She made fun of Huddles for getting left

back, too. She called us all a bunch of losers," said Stevie, his eyes bright with anger.

"I hate her," I said, hoping to win points. It didn't work.

"That's a white school, huh?" Huddles wanted to know.

"No! It's actually a green-and-blue school," I joked.

Nobody laughed.

"Any black kids there?" Kenny stared right in my face.

"They had this guy named Ronald Walker last year—" I began.

"Awww, man!" they said in unison.

"You're going to be the only brother in the whole school? You'll definitely turn white!" said Stevie.

"Impossible!" I yelled. "How can a black kid turn white?"

"Easy," said Huddles. "You'll start talking white and acting white."

"And dressing white," added Stevie.

"You'll be an Oreo," said Kenny.

"A *what*?"

"Black on the outside and white on the inside. Like an Oreo cookie!" said Kenny.

"Look who's talking! You think you're Chinese. You wear kung fu slippers and clothes from Chinatown! You even *speak* Chinese!"

Kenny was fuming. I could almost see steam coming off the top of his head. I sensed his weak spot and hit harder.

"You're a phony. Face it. You're not even that good at karate!"

"You better chill out, Drew," said Stevie, stepping between us.

"No! Show me some of your moves, Bruce Lee! I'll prove to you right now I'm no white boy!"

Kenny threw up his hands and began making a bizarre, high-pitched sound.

"*Waii eee aiiee!*" he wailed, his teeth bared. Stevie and Huddles jumped back as Kenny waved his arms wildly. "*Wo-xiang-zou-ni!*" he screamed, which I figured translated to "I'm going to kick your Oreo butt." I put up both hands like Mike Tyson and moved in. Kenny backed away, wailing and making complicated kung fu gestures. Stevie and Huddles watched, mesmerized, as he showed off his technique.

Much to Kenny's surprise, I was not

impressed. I threw out a left jab and grazed his right ear. As he covered his ear, wincing, I punched him square in the nose with a right cross. Then I jumped him, pinning him to the asphalt.

40

I punched him wildly in his exposed mid-section as he covered his face. He tried kicking me off, but he couldn't. Stevie grabbed me around my waist to pull me off, and I spun around and hit him in the eye with my elbow. He cried out and fell to the ground, holding his face.

Kenny caught me in the jaw with an uppercut and I fell off him. Huddles pulled me up off the ground by my shirt collar with tears in his eyes. "Get out of here, Drew!" he cried, shoving me away.

I felt my bottom lip and saw blood on my fingers. Huddles and Stevie helped Kenny up. He was bent over, holding his face in his hands.

"I said *get out of here!*" Huddles yelled again. I turned and ran home, my heart pounding in my heaving chest. For a guy who had just won a big fight, I sure felt like a loser.

Chapter

7

The fight between me and my three friends was nothing compared to the screaming match between Jessie and me.

Fortunately my folks were at Drummond, meeting with Kyle's principal. They weren't home to see me return from school filthy and bleeding from the mouth.

Jessie met me at the front door as I fumbled for my key.

"Ohmigod! What happened to you?" she gasped.

"Got in a fight."

"Ohmigod!" she said again. She ran to the kitchen and came back with a damp dish towel. As she handed it to me, I blurted, "This is all your fault, Jessie!"

"Are you deranged?" she cried. Jessie never uses common words like other people. She'd never say someone was crazy when she could use a fancier word like *deranged*.

"You told my friends about Deerwood!"

"So what? Are you ashamed of going there?"

"I don't 'go' to Deerwood," I shouted. "I haven't taken one test yet, and already everybody at Hamilton and Drummond knows all about it! You have the biggest, stupidest mouth in the world!"

"You're a spoiled little brat, you know that?" she said, waving a skinny finger at me.

"Spoiled?"

"You get everything you want! You should be happy about Deerwood!"

Suddenly she got calm and rational, which I hate. "Face it," she said. "Those homeboys of yours won't ever amount to anything. Good thing you're done with them."

"I'm not 'done' with anybody—except *you*!"

"Please," she said matter-of-factly. "You're going to make new friends. Rich, white friends."

"I am *not* going to make any new friends! In fact, I'll probably fail their stupid tests anyway!"

"You're not making sense," Jessie said. "You are incomprehensible." While I was wondering what that meant, she took back the dish towel.

"By the way," she said, dabbing at my bloody lip. "Who did you get into a fight with?"

"Everybody." I sighed. The dish towel felt good. "Stevie, Kenny, Huddles."

"You fought three guys? Did you win?"

"I think I broke Kenny's nose. Stevie's got a black eye. And Huddles can't stand the sight of me."

"So you *did* win!" She beamed.

Chapter

8

Fat Ernie spent the end of the school year plotting revenge against Kyle. But Kyle wasn't around Drummond much. After he was suspended for fighting, Dad loaded him down with chores. He had to come straight home from school every day to do them. Not only that, Dad drove him to and from school just to make sure he kept out of trouble.

Good thing Fat Ernie was stupid. He couldn't resist showing off his gun, and shot a squirrel in the tail to impress Rock and Crazy Cecil. The squirrel survived, but a plainclothes policeman arrested Ernie. He was shipped upstate to a school for troubled youth two weeks before graduation.

As graduation day came closer I got unhappier and unhappier. I was lonelier than I'd ever been in my life. I never saw my friends anymore. Stevie hadn't even returned my latest Mason Stone comic book—Adventure #10.

I graduated on a perfect sunny afternoon, surrounded by happy, smiling people. But my own mood was dark.

If only Hamilton went up to the twelfth grade, I thought. *I wouldn't have these problems.* I browsed through our yearbook, looking at the goofy graduation photos. I was stunned when I stumbled onto a page of Mason Stone sketches. The caption under them read, "Drew Taylor is the gifted creator of *Mason Stone, Superagent*. We're sorry to see you go, Drew. You'll be missed." How had Mr. Taffer gotten the drawings? And had he written the caption?

"Nice drawings, bro." Kyle's voice broke into my thoughts.

"Uh . . . thanks. I didn't even know they'd be in here."

"Nice yearbook, too," he said, touching

the leather. "Much nicer than anything at Drummond."

"You all right about keeping on there?" I asked, straightening his tie. Even though Jessie and I were changing schools, Kyle would be staying at Drummond.

"I like it all right," Kyle said. "And I'm used to it. I wouldn't adjust well to a new school."

"Sounds like something Dad would say."

"Dad's right. I wouldn't adjust well to new rules. It's taken me two years to get to know Drummond."

"Smile, Drew!" Mom and Dad were back, pointing a camera at me.

"Can I sign your yearbook?" It was Candace, a girl who used to pass me notes earlier in the school year. She loved the fact that I could draw. "And would you draw Mason Stone in mine?"

I quickly dashed off a sketch for her.

I should charge her a dollar, I thought, signing my name.

She handed me my yearbook, giggling, and ran off to her parents.

I looked in my book. I was horrified to see that she had used a whole blank page to scrawl "Have a great summer. Love, Candace," with a goofy smiling face next to it.

There were only two other signatures in the book, and they both said that exact thing: "Have a great summer."

I knew I wouldn't.

I posed for a bunch of photos and didn't smile for any of them. There wasn't much to smile about. I barely caught a glimpse of Stevie. He and Kenny rode away in the backseat of a relative's car, right after the ceremony. I didn't even have a chance to ask for my comic book back.

Chapter

9

Summer came, but I was too busy taking tests for Deerwood to notice. I took six: two in hot, vacant classrooms of Hamilton Elementary, two in the basement of my church, and two at Deerwood.

I didn't study for the exams. Deep down I hoped to fail them. I knew that I'd have a better chance of getting back together with Stevie, Kenny, and Huddles if I didn't pass.

I had completely lost contact with them. Stevie and Kenny were still hanging out together, and Huddles was gone—sent down South to stay with his uncle. Jessie told me she'd heard it from Huddles's sister.

In July I got more bad news. I had won entry into Deerwood. Worse news came a week later. One of my tests was for an academic scholarship, and I had won that, too.

Now I *really* had to go to Deerwood.

My family went crazy when they heard. Mom came running to the house waving a letter in the air. I thought we had won the clearinghouse sweepstakes!

"It's official!" she screamed. "Come quickly!"

Everybody rushed into the kitchen to hear what the excitement was about.

"Drew won the scholarship!" she exclaimed, fighting back tears.

"You did it, boy!" said Kyle, smiling from ear to ear. It was the biggest, toothiest grin I had seen on his face in a long time.

"Son, this is the proudest day of our lives," said Dad, looking teary-eyed.

Even Jessie was moved in her own way. Her mouth hung open and she was speechless. That was a real first.

A week later, I was fitted for a green blazer with antlers embroidered on the pocket. When I saw myself in the mirror wearing the blazer, something amazing happened.

I turned white!

As I stood in Dr. Barnett's wood-paneled office wearing the blazer, my reflection changed—slowly.

First, my hair turned blond. Then it straightened and fell over my forehead. Next, my features narrowed. I looked at my hands in the mirror. They were white too! "Oh, no!" I said to myself. "My friends were right. I've turned into a white kid!"

I turned to face Dr. Barnett. He was more thrilled than ever.

"Perfect!" he said. "Welcome, Drew, to the Deerwood School for Boys!"

When I stepped outside, my mood was dark, just like the rain clouds that hovered over my blond head. I decided to make a run for the train station before the clouds burst, but it was too late. I was caught in a fierce downpour. I tried to use the plastic bag that protected my new blazer as an umbrella. It didn't work. The wind blew the bag out of my hands, and I had to run in the wrong direction to get it back.

It poured steadily throughout the long train ride. It didn't slack up any as I stood waiting for the bus, so I walked home.

How perfect! I thought. *Miserable weather for the most miserable day of my life!* I caught my reflection in a car window as I trudged through the rain. I was still white. *Well, at least I can walk down my block without anyone seeing me like this.*

Nobody will be outside in this weather.

By the time I reached my house, I was completely drenched. All my clothing was soaked, except for the dry blazer under the plastic bag.

When I opened my front door, Jessie was there waiting. Arms crossed, she glared at me.

"Where were you?" she snapped. My color must have changed back to normal, since she made no mention of it. "You're soaked!"

"I had to pick up my school uniform." I showed her the long plastic bag slung over my shoulder.

"Well, this mail came for you," she said. She thrust two envelopes at me. One was letter-size. The other was a big brown envelope. I didn't recognize the writing on either one.

"Open them," she said eagerly.

"It's personal."

"How do you know until you see what's inside?"

56

"Can I get out of these wet clothes first? I'll read the mail later."

Jessie stormed away in a huff, and I climbed the stairs to my room.

I stuffed the envelopes under my pillow and found some dry clothes. I was so wet, I stood in the bathtub to peel my clothes off.

I put on a sweatshirt, jeans, and dry socks and went back downstairs.

Everybody in the family was in the living room waiting for me when I returned.

"Well? Where is it, son?" asked Dad.

"Where is what?" I asked, puzzled.

"The blazer, Drew!" exclaimed Mom. "We want to see how it looks on you!"

"Um, it looks fine," I mumbled. "I tried it on already."

"Everybody wants to see it on, doofus," said Jessie.

"I don't want to wear it right now, okay?" I shot in Jessie's direction.

I turned around and went back upstairs to hide in my room. I knew I was hurting everyone's feelings, but I needed to be alone. How could I celebrate with my family? I'd lost my best friends over this new school! For the first time in years I wanted to cry.

The crunch of the envelopes under my pillow surprised me. I had forgotten about the two letters. I decided to open the big envelope first.

It was my comic book. The messages on the back helped me to fall asleep—with a smile on my face.

DREW TAYLOR presents

MASON STONE SUPERAGENT

STONE sheds his TRENCHCOAT for the most DANGEROUS MISSION OF HIS LIFE!

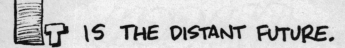**T** IS THE DISTANT FUTURE.

THE WORLD HAS BEEN RIPPED APART BY WAR, DISEASE, AND **TOXIC WASTE**

CIVILIZATION EXISTS IN A BIO-METRO-SPHERE KNOWN AS **THE CAPITAL**

ONE EXILED MADMAN LIVING INSIDE A MOUNTAIN FORTRESS PLOTS TO TERMINATE LIFE ON PLANET **EARTH**

HE IS EVIL. HE IS FEARED. HE IS **XTINCTION**

THE END

Awesome! The
best one
ever!
Your friend 4 Life,
Stevie

Drew, you are still
THE MAN! Kenny

FROM ATLANTA!

P.S. HUDDLES IS GOING TO CALL YOU →

The second envelope made me feel rich!